Mushroom in the Rain

Adapted from the Russian of V. Suteyev

By Mirra Ginsburg

Pictures by Jose Aruego & Ariane Dewey

Macmillan Publishing Company

New York

10 9 8 7 6 5 4

The text was adapted from the Russian *Pod Gribom* (Under the Mushroom) of V. Suteyev.
The four-color illustrations were prepared as pen-and-ink line drawings with halftone overlays.
The typeface is Photo Plantin.
The Library of Congress has cataloged the first printing of this title as follows:
Ginsburg, Mirra.   Mushroom in the rain.   [1. Animals—Stories. 2. Mushrooms—Stories]
I. Suteyev, Vladimir Grigor'evich. Pod gribom. II. Aruego, Jose, illus. III. Dewey, Ariane, illus. IV. Title.
PZ10.3.G455Mu   [E]   72-92438   ISBN 0-02-736241-8

To Juan–J.A.

One day an ant was caught in the rain.
"Where can I hide?" he wondered.

He saw a tiny mushroom peeking out of
the ground in a clearing, and he hid under it.
He sat there, waiting for the rain to stop.
But the rain came down harder and harder.

A wet butterfly crawled up to the mushroom.

"Cousin Ant, let me come in from the rain.

I am so wet I cannot fly."

"How can I let you in?" said the ant.

"There is barely room enough for one."

"It does not matter," said the butterfly.

"Better crowded than wet."

The ant moved over and made room for the butterfly.

The rain came down harder and harder.

A mouse ran up.

"Let me in under the mushroom.

I am drenched to the bone."

"How can we let you in? There is no more room here."

"Just move a little closer!"

They huddled closer and let the mouse in.

And the rain came down and came down and would not stop.

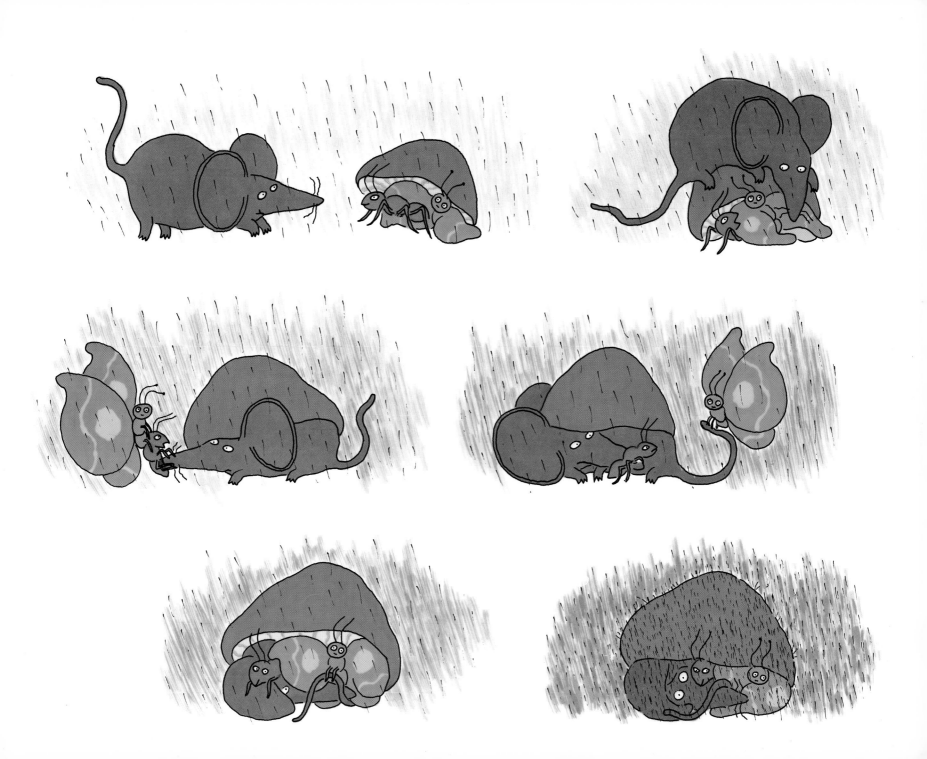

A little sparrow hopped up to the mushroom, crying:
"My feathers are dripping, my wings are so tired!
   Let me in under the mushroom to dry out
   and rest until the rain stops!"
"But there is no room here."
"Please! Move over just a little!"
   They moved over, and there was
   room enough for the sparrow.

Then a rabbit hopped into the clearing
  and saw the mushroom.
"Oh, hide me!" he cried. "Save me! A fox is chasing me!"
"Poor rabbit," said the ant. "Let's crowd ourselves
  a little more and take him in."

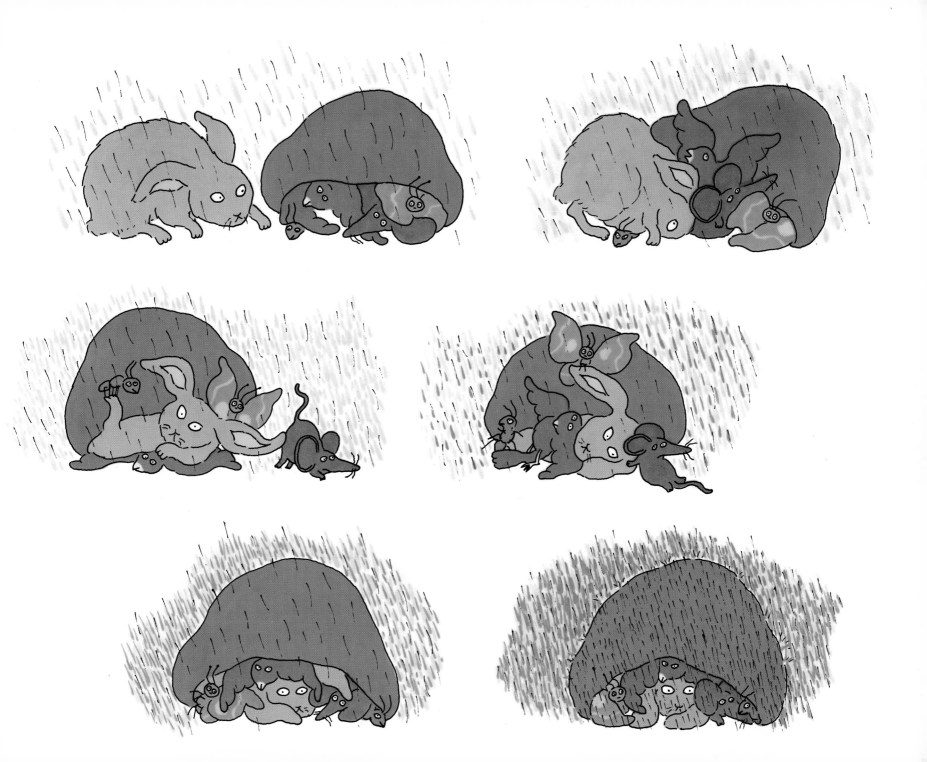

As soon as they hid the rabbit, the fox came running.

"Have you seen the rabbit? Which way did he go?" he asked.

"We have not seen him."

The fox came nearer and sniffed.

"There is a rabbit smell around. Isn't he hiding here?"

"You silly fox! How could a rabbit get in here?

Don't you see there isn't any room?"

The fox turned up his nose, flicked his tail, and ran off.

By then the rain was over.
The sun looked out from behind the clouds.
And everyone came out from under
the mushroom, bright and merry.

The ant looked at his neighbors.
"How could this be? At first I had hardly room enough
under the mushroom just for myself, and in the end
all five of us were able to sit under it."

"Qua-ha-ha! Qua-ha-ha!" somebody laughed loudly behind them.
They turned and saw a fat green frog sitting on top
of the mushroom, shaking his head at them.
"Qua-ha-ha!" said the frog. "Don't you know
what happens to a mushroom in the rain?"
And he hopped away, still laughing.

The ant, the butterfly, the mouse, the sparrow, and
the rabbit looked at one another, then at the mushroom.
And suddenly they knew why there was room enough
under the mushroom for them all.

Do you know?

Can you guess what happens to a mushroom when it rains?

IT GROWS!